For young James (N)

Copyright © 1994 by Jill Newton
First published in Great Britain by ABC, All Books for Children,
a division of The All Children's Company, Ltd., 33 Museum Street, London WC1 A 1LD.
All rights reserved. No part of this book may be reproduced or utilized in any form or
by any means, electronic or mechanical, including photocopying and recording, or
by any information storage and retrieval system, without permission in writing from
the Publisher. Inquiries should be addressed to Lothrop, Lee & Shepard Books,
a division of William Morrow & Company, Inc., 1350 Avenue of the Americas,
New York, New York 10019
First U.S. Edition 1 2 3 4 5 6 7 8 9 10
Printed in Hong Kong
Library of Congress Cataloging in Publication Data
Newton, Jill, Don't sit there! / by Jill Newton.
p.   cm.   Summary: Things begin disappearing after a family's sofa is
delivered. ISBN 0-688-13309-6 [1. Family life—Fiction.]   I. Title. PZ7.N48674Do
1994 [E]—dc20 93-23538 CIP AC

Don't Sit There!

Jill Newton

Lothrop, Lee & Shepard Books   New York

Fat Aunt Marilyn came to see us and broke
the sofa. Suddenly, there she was, legs waving
in the air, and the sofa in pieces all around her.
   My sister, Em, said, "Question: What time
is it when fat Aunt Marilyn sits on the sofa?
Answer: Time to get a new sofa!"
   Aunt Marilyn scowled and Mom scolded.

I went with Mom to get a new sofa. We were having a birthday party for Grandma, and needed one right away. We looked for hours and hours. I was tired and sat down to wait.

The sofa I was sitting on was so
comfortable, I almost fell asleep.
Mom thought it was comfortable,
too, and bought it.

Two large men brought our sofa home. They put it in the living room, huffing and puffing and complaining how heavy it was. I heard Dad telling Mom that they just wanted a tip.

As soon as they'd moved it this way and moved it that way and put it where the old one had been, we all took turns sitting on it.

"I could get lost in a sofa like this," said Em.

Dad went to get some money to give them
their tip, but the men had gone.

Even Brian, the cat, thought I'd made a good choice. He curled up and went to sleep, until our dog, Ralph, jumped up and they started fighting. Mom yelled at them like she always does, and they were soon gone, probably outside, to keep fighting.

Just then Grandma came in from one
of her walks. She liked the sofa, too.

"Oh, it reminds me of one we used to have when I was a girl," she said, sitting down. She started to tell Mom and me about when she was a little girl, and I crept upstairs.

When I came down later, Grandma was gone. "I don't know where she got to," Mom said when I asked. "I went to answer the phone and she just disappeared."

"Disappeared? Who's disappeared?" said my brother, Keith, as he dropped his cassette player on the sofa.

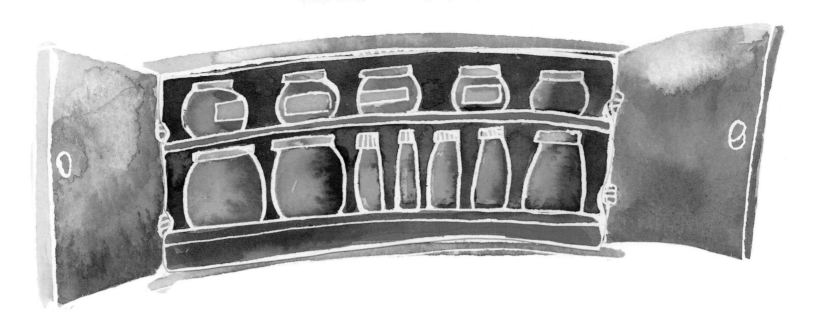

"Grandma," said Mom. "I hope she hasn't forgotten
it's her birthday. Come on," she said, turning to me. "Help
me put the icing on her cake."
I had just picked up the cake when the doorbell
rang. "I'll get it – it might be Grandma!"

My brother was crawling around the living
room floor. "Did you take my cassette player?" he asked.
"No! And don't touch this cake," I told him, putting
it on the sofa. When I got back from letting my cousin
Franklin in, Dad was looking for his briefcase.
"I'm sure I left it here."
"Did someone let Ralph in?"
I asked. "Grandma's birthday
cake is gone!"

B r r r i n g   The doorbell started ringing again.

It was Aunt Marilyn.

Before anyone could stop her, she took one
look at the new sofa and, "OOOOH!"
plonked herself down.

With a huge crash, our comfortable
new sofa splintered into pieces and,
once again, fat Aunt Marilyn
was on the floor.

And there, from where they'd disappeared
into the sofa, came the two large men who
had delivered it to us, Ralph, Brian, my
brother's cassette player, Dad's briefcase,
the birthday cake, and — Grandma!

"Happy Birthday, Grandma!" we all said.